30p

This
Christmas Cracker
belongs to:

_____

_____

First published 1986 by Walker Books Ltd
87 Vauxhall Walk, London SE11 5HJ
This edition published 2010
2 4 6 8 10 9 7 5 3 1
Text © 1986 Sarah Hayes
Illustrations © 1986 Jamie Charteris
The right of Sarah Hayes and Jamie Charteris to be identified as
author and illustrator respectively of this work has been asserted by them
in accordance with the Copyright, Designs and Patents Act 1988
Printed in China
British Library Cataloguing in Publication Data:
a catalogue record for this book is available from the British Library
978-1-4063-3307-7
www.walker.co.uk

A Bad Start for Father Christmas

Illustrated by
Sarah Hayes

Illustrated by
Jamie Charteris

WALKER BOOKS

AND SUBSIDIARIES

LONDON · BOSTON · SYDNEY · AUCKLAND

Father Christmas woke up late.
He looked out of the window.
It was snowing.
It was always snowing.

'Christmas Eve today,' said Father Christmas.
He jumped out of bed and touched his toes.
Under his bed he could see a toy car.

'Someone might like that,' he said, and he
put the car into his spare sack.

He went into the
bathroom to wash his
face and brush his teeth.

When he pulled back
the shower curtain, he
was surprised to find a
large drum.

'My gnomes are getting
careless,' Father Christmas
said. He tapped the drum
with his toothbrush and
dropped it into the sack.

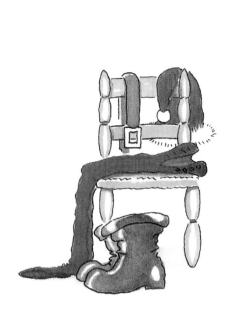

Then he put on his clothes: red pants, a long
white shirt, a red jacket and hat trimmed with
fur and an enormous pair of red trousers.

'Now for the boots,' he said. 'Perhaps I ought
to have new boots next year.'

'I need a good breakfast today,' said Father Christmas. 'It's my special day.' He went into the kitchen and made himself a huge breakfast.

'It's getting late,' he said, and ate his breakfast very quickly. Someone had left a teddy bear in the cupboard. Father Christmas put it in his sack.

Then he remembered something he had forgotten.

'My mittens!' he cried. 'Where are my mittens? I can't go without them.'

He felt in his jacket pockets, but they weren't there. He felt in his front trouser pockets, but they weren't there either.

'Bother!' said Father Christmas. 'I'll have to search the place, and I'm late already.'

He took the lift down to the workshop.

'Have you seen my mittens?' he asked the gnome who worked the lift.

'No, F.C.,' said the gnome, 'but I did find something in the lift yesterday.' He held out a wind-up mouse. Father Christmas dropped the mouse into his sack.

In the workshop the gnomes were busy.

Father Christmas had to shout.

'I can't find my mittens!' he roared. But the gnomes were too busy to pay any attention to him. And they were too busy to see a small doll by the lift.

'You look lost,' said Father Christmas and he put the doll gently into the sack.

The next place to visit was the paintshop.
Father Christmas knocked on the door.
It opened a crack and a jet of blue paint
shot past and landed on the wall.

'Sorry F.C.,' said a gnome with blue hands
and face. 'What can we do for you?'

'I'm looking for my mittens,' said
Father Christmas. 'They're red.'

'I know that,' said the gnome.
'They're not here,' he added,
'and if they were, they'd
be blue now.' He handed
Father Christmas a bright
blue trumpet and shut
the door.

'Sweet factory next,'
said Father Christmas.
It was his favourite
place. One of the
gnomes gave him a
stick of rock.

'I'm too full to eat it now,' he said.
'I'll put it into my sack for safe keeping.'
Then he shouted above the noise,
'Has anyone seen my mittens?'
But no one answered.

Father Christmas was getting worried.

'I might have left my mittens in the packing room,' he said. 'Perhaps they've been wrapped up by mistake.' When he put his nose round the door, all he could see was a mountain of paper and ribbon and sticky tape.

'Mittens?' he said hopefully. 'Red mittens?' One of the gnomes emerged from the mountain.

'All mittens are stripy this year,' he said. 'No plain
mittens at all. Not plain blue, not plain green, not
plain yellow—'

'And not plain red,' interrupted Father Christmas.
'Oh dear.' Then he saw a bag of chocolate coins on
the floor. 'That doesn't need wrapping,' he said,
'and it shouldn't be on the floor.'

The store room had boxes full of presents stacked
up to the ceiling, all neatly labelled. Father Christmas
caught sight of something red behind one of the stacks,
but it was only a yo-yo.

'This hasn't got a label,' he said to the storekeeper.

'Oh, take it away,' said the storekeeper.
'I don't know what to do with it.'

Father Christmas looked at his watch.
'There's not much time left,' he said.
'Where can those mittens have gone?'
Then he had an idea. He hurried along the
corridor and unbolted the boiler room door.

He switched on the light and
went carefully down the steps.
'No mittens in here,'
said Father Christmas after
searching for a few minutes.
He scrambled up the steps
and slipped on a
shiny whistle which
lay on the top step.
'What a place to
leave it,' he said.

Now it was time to feed the reindeers.
After the boiler room the stable felt very cold.
Father Christmas clapped his hands together
to warm them up.

'Bother those mittens!' he said. 'Where can they be?'
He gave the reindeers an extra large dinner.

'Do you know where my mittens are?' he asked.
The reindeers munched their hay and didn't answer.
'Of course you don't,' said Father Christmas.
A bright yellow ball lay on top of one of the hay racks.
'We really are very untidy this year,' said Father
Christmas crossly, and he put the ball into his sack.

The last place to look
was the shed where
Father Christmas
kept his sledge.
Two gnomes
were polishing
the paintwork.

The gnomes gasped.
One of them jumped
into the sledge.
  'Perhaps they're down
behind the seat,' he said.
'There's something here.'

'What is it? Let me see!' shouted Father
Christmas. The gnome held up a painted fan.
'Oh,' said Father Christmas. 'Oh dear.'
He put the fan into his sack and
walked slowly back to the house.
The sack was very
heavy now.

Father Christmas slumped down in an armchair in the hall. He felt miserable.

'Next year we shall have to be more organised,' he said. 'If there is a next year,' he added gloomily.

At that moment a group of gnomes came rushing up in a panic.

'We're the counters,' said one lot of gnomes.
'And we're the checkers,' said the other lot.
'And we're one sack short!' they all shouted
together. 'We haven't enough presents
to go round.'

'And I can't drive the sledge because I can't
find my mittens,' said Father Christmas.

'Your mittens are in your back pockets, F.C.,'
said one of the counters. 'That's where you
always put them.' Father Christmas stood up.
He felt in his back pocket, and there was
one red mitten. He felt in his
other pocket, and there was a
second red mitten.
Father Christmas smiled
a big smile.

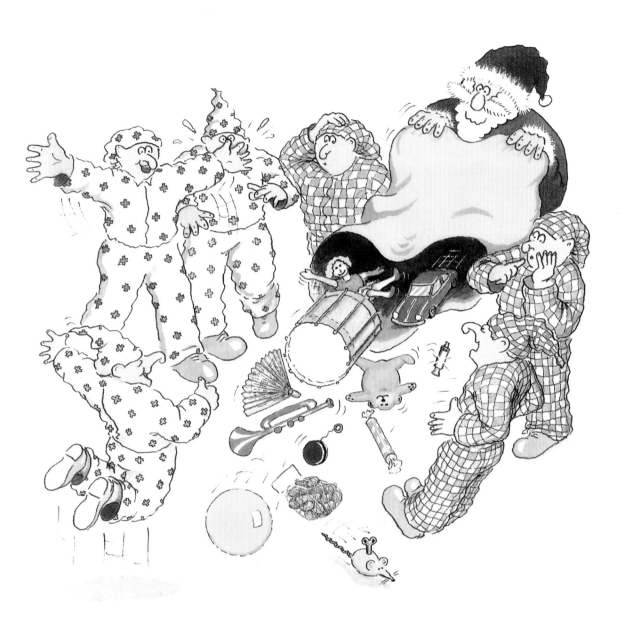

'You have solved my problem,' he said, 'and I think
I can solve yours. Is this what you are looking for?'
  The gnomes were amazed. They all spoke at once.
'How did you…? Where on earth…?
Where did you find them?'

'Oh, all over the place,' said Father
Christmas. 'In the bedroom, in the
bathroom, in the kitchen, in the lift,

in the workshop, in the paintshop, in the sweet factory,
in the packing room, in the store room, in the
boiler room, in the stable, in the shed…'

'And in the hall,' cried one of the gnomes,
holding up a toy boat he had found under
Father Christmas's chair.

'And now,' said Father Christmas,

'I really must be off, or I shall be late.
One minute to go.'
  He picked up the sack, put on his big
red mittens, and went outside.

The snow had stopped.
'It's going to be a fine night after all,' said
Father Christmas and he sped off into the darkness.
'Merry Christmas!' shouted the gnomes, but
Father Christmas was too far away
to hear them.